WELCOME TO PASSPORT TO READING

A beginning reader's ticket to a brand-new world!

Every book in this program is designed to build read-along and read-alone skills, level by level, through engaging and enriching stories. As the reader turns each page, he or she will become more confident with new vocabulary, sight words, and comprehension.

These PASSPORT TO READING levels will help you choose the perfect book for every reader.

READING TOGETHER
Read short words in simple sentence structures together to begin a reader's journey.

READING OUT LOUD
Encourage developing readers to sound out words in more complex stories with simple vocabulary.

READING INDEPENDENTLY
Newly independent readers gain confidence reading more complex sentences with higher word counts.

READY TO READ MORE
Readers prepare for chapter books with fewer illustrations and longer paragraphs.

This book features sight words from the educator-supported Dolch Sight Words List. This encourages the reader to recognize commonly used vocabulary words, increasing reading speed and fluency.

For more information, please visit passporttoreadingbooks.com.

Enjoy the journey!

Cover design by Elaine Lopez-Levine.

Little, Brown and Company
Hachette Book Group
1290 Avenue of the Americas, New York, NY 10104
Visit us at LBYR.com
enchantimals.com

First Edition: September 2018

Little, Brown and Company is a division of Hachette Book Group, Inc.
The Little, Brown name and logo are trademarks of Hachette Book Group, Inc.

Library of Congress Control Number: 2018936332

ISBN: 978-0-316-41908-6 (pbk.)

Printed in the United States of America

CW

10 9 8 7 6 5 4 3 2 1

Passport to Reading titles are leveled by independent reviewers applying the standards developed by Irene Fountas and Gay Su Pinnell in *Matching Books to Readers: Using Leveled Books in Guided Reading*, Heinemann, 1999.

MEET THE Enchantimals™

Perdita Finn
Based on the screenplay written by Douglas Wood

LB
LITTLE, BROWN AND COMPANY
New York Boston

**Hello, Enchantimals friends!
Look for these words when you read
this book. Can you spot them all?**

cottage

carrot

wiggle

den

New friends have come to Wonderwood.
Welcome, Patter Peacock and Flap!
Flap is Patter's bestie.

The Enchantimals and their besties are excited to show Patter and Flap around Wonderwood.

There is so much to see! Where will they go first?

Sage Skunk giggles.
Sage and Caper's
cottage is so pretty.

Sage is in a band!
She can play lots of instruments.
She likes to sing.

Her bestie, Caper,
goes crazy on the drums.

Patter wants to be in the band, too.
Sage is so excited!
She and Caper high-five each other
with their tails.
But the music is too loud for Flap!

Bree Bunny and her bestie, Twist, thump their feet. Patter and Flap are coming for breakfast!

Bree and Twist love to cook.
Their favorite ingredient is carrot!

Bree invented a special
carrot cake machine.
Yum!

Bree and Twist go out to the garden.
They dig up carrots for the cake!
Do Patter and Flap like carrots?
Oops—Bree and Twist forgot to ask!

Patter and Flap head over
to Felicity Fox's den.
She lives there with her bestie, Flick.

Felicity and Flick are looking
at a map of Everwilde.
They are trying to find Junglewood.
That is where Patter and Flap
come from.

But now Patter and Flap want
to live in Wonderwood forever.
Felicity and Flick wiggle their ears.
They are so happy!

Felicity and Flick invite Patter
and Flap to stay in their den.
But their den is too dark for peacocks.

Luckily, Danessa Deer's cabin
is very sunny.
It is surrounded by flowers.
Lots of flowers.

Inside the cabin are even more flowers.
Danessa and her bestie, Sprint,
have flowers all over!

Danessa and Sprint make a special bouquet for Patter and Flap.

ACHOO! Uh-oh!

The flowers are making Flap sneeze!

Where will Patter and Flap live?
Danessa has an idea.
Danessa loves to help.

The Enchantimals will find Patter and Flap their own home.

Patter does not want a house
that is too loud or too dark
or makes her bestie sneeze
or has a garden full of carrots like Bree's.

She DOES want a house full of her and Flap's favorite things.

After all, Felicity has her books,

and Sage has her musical instruments.

Patter and Flap go to the Babbling Brook.

It is a good place to think.

All the animals have a place to live.

A caterpillar has a cocoon.

A bird has a nest.

A turtle has a shell.

Where will Patter and Flap live?

Felicity and Flick scamper to find Patter and Flap.

The Enchantimals have found the perfect house for their new friends.

Danessa is so relieved!

She and Sprint tap their antlers!

Hooray!

The Enchantimals work together to
make the house perfect for Patter and Flap.
Bree plants raspberry bushes.
Felicity adds a peacock design to the roof.

Sage paints the walls blue.
Danessa adds pretty pillows.
Will Patter and Flap like their
new home?

YES—they love it!

The pair flutter their wings together.

Flap sings and Patter joins in.

They are home in Wonderwood at last!